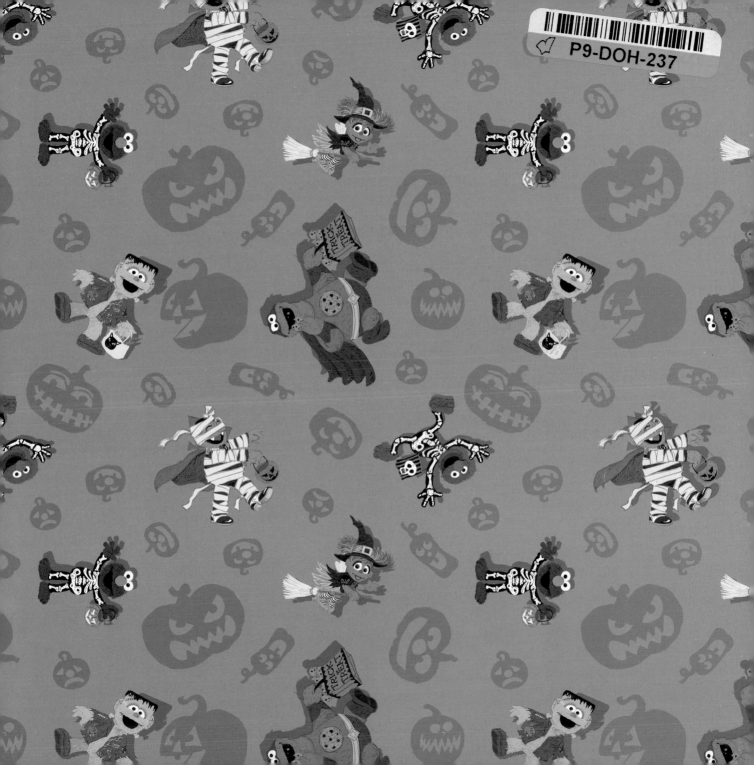

HAPPY HALLOWEEN!

By Lillian Jaine

Illustrated by Ernie Kwiat

sourcebooks jabberwocky

SESAME STREET

Once upon a Halloween creepy,
the Count was getting rather sleepy.

TAP!

TAP!

TAP!

While he nodded, nearly napping,
suddenly there came a tapping,
as of someone gently rapping at his castle door.

"A visitor!" he cried with glee.
"I think they'd like some treats from me!"

But when he looked outside his door,
he saw darkness there, and nothing more.

"Trick or treat!" a small voice cried.
The Count jumped up in great surprise.

"Elmo? Is that you I see?"
"It is!" said Elmo. "Happy Halloween!"

"Come in, come in," the Count invited.
"My first guest. I'm so excited!"

But only seconds passed before they heard
one tap, two taps, and then a third!

TAP!
TAP!
TAP!

When they took a glance outside,
a frightening sight met both their eyes.

"A ghost! A ghost!" they cried with fear.
"Not me!" they heard. "There's no ghost here!"

Then Elmo noticed something more.
He knew he'd seen those feet before!

"Big Bird?" he asked. "Could it be you?"
"Yes, it's me!" he shouted. "Boo!"

Again the door closed with a snap.
Again they heard that *tap, tap, tap!*

"A trick-or-treater?" Elmo wondered.
The Count looked scared. The black sky thundered.

TAP! TAP! TAP!

Through the window they took a peek,
and what they saw made them shout, "EEK!"

A bony creature gazed at them.
"Oh no!" they cried. "A skeleton!"

The creature smiled, took off his mask.
The Count couldn't help but gasp.

"Grover!" he said with relief.
"Thank goodness it's just make-believe!"

More friends arrived to trick or treat,
and every costume looked quite neat.

"Come in," Count said, "come everyone!"
"Let's all have some spooky fun!"

And now the night was in full swing.
The Count had planned for everything.

But then, "Oh no!" a loud voice cried.
"I hear a tapping from outside!"

Another guest? Count worried, wondered.
Again, outside, the black sky thundered.

He looked around, then looked again.
All ten friends were there with him.

A monster, a pumpkin, a ghost, and a cat.
Pirates, a robot, a witch in a hat.
There was the knight, the skeleton too!
So who was tapping? Nobody knew!

Tap, tap, tap, they heard once more.
Then they gathered at the door.

Deep into that darkness peering,
long they stood there wondering, fearing.

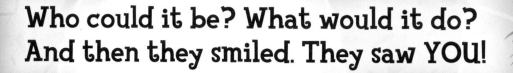

Who could it be? What would it do?
And then they smiled. They saw YOU!

"Hooray! You're here!" said everyone.
"Happy Halloween! Come join the fun!"

Cover and internal design © 2014 by Sourcebooks, Inc.
Cover illustrations © Sesame Workshop
Cover design by Jason Lavicky
Text by Lillian Jaine
Illustrations by Ernie Kwiat

Published by Sourcebooks Jabberwocky, an imprint of Sourcebooks, Inc.
P.O. Box 4410, Naperville, Illinois 60567-4410
(630) 961-3900
Fax: (630) 961-2168
www.jabberwockykids.com

Library of Congress Cataloging-in-Publication data is on file with the publisher

Source of Production: Leo Paper, Heshan City, Guangdong Province, China
Date of Production: June 2017
Run Number: 5009618

Printed and bound in China.
LEO 10 9 8 7 6